This is Builder Bill with his bricks
and his mortar (to stick the bricks).
He is a very good builder, and his
houses never fall down.

A catalogue record for this book is available from the British Library

Published by Ladybird Books Ltd
80 Strand London WC2R 0RL
A Penguin Company

8 10 9

Little Workmates

Builder Bill

by Mandy Ross

illustrated by Emma Dodd

Ladybird

Builder Bill woke up early. "I've got to finish Mrs Dogsberry's house today," he said. "I hope she'll like it."

Builder Bill whistled
on his way to work.

"There's lots to do
before Mrs Dogsberry
arrives," he said.

Builder Bill whistled as he mixed some mortar.

"There we go – last few bricks..." he said, laying them straight.

Builder Bill whistled as he climbed up his ladder.

"There we go – last few roof tiles..." he said, holding on tight.

Builder Bill whistled as he opened a pot of paint.

"There we go — bright red front door..." he said, trying not to drip.

Just as he finished,
Mrs Dogsberry arrived with
her dog, Barker.

Builder Bill showed them
around the house.

"Perfect!" said
Mrs Dogsberry.
"But...

what about Barker?"

"Don't worry," said Builder Bill,
"I haven't forgotten
about him."

"Woof!" barked Barker.

"There's lots more to do,"
said Builder Bill.

He whistled as he mixed
some mortar and started
building again...

"There we go—last few
bricks..." said Builder Bill.
"Last few roof tiles...
bright red front door..."

"Finished!" called Builder Bill.
"There we go – your new
kennel, Barker!"

"Perfect," said
Mrs Dogsberry.

"Thank you,
Builder Bill."

"Two more satisfied customers," smiled Builder Bill, and he whistled as he drove home for his tea.

"I hope Mrs Dogsberry and Barker sleep well tonight," he thought.

This is Fireman Fergus. He is a brave firefighter and he has a good head for heights. Fireman Fergus has a cat called Tibbles to whom he tells all his Fireman's adventures.

This is Nurse Nancy. She is always neat and tidy and she works very hard looking after the patients at Story Town Hospital.

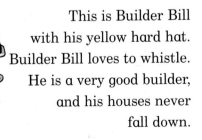

This is Builder Bill with his yellow hard hat. Builder Bill loves to whistle. He is a very good builder, and his houses never fall down.